The Pied Piper of Hamelin

PICTURE WINDOW BOOKS
a capstone imprint

First published in the United States in 2011
by Picture Window Books
A Capstone Imprint
151 Good Counsel Drive
P.O. Box 669
Mankato, Minnesota 56002
www.capstonepub.com

Library of Congress Cataloging-in-Publication Data is available on the Library of Congress website.
ISBN 978-1-4048-6501-3 (library binding)

Summary: A pied piper rids the city of Hamelin of rats in this retelling of the classic tale.

Art Director: Kay Fraser
Graphic Designer: Emily Harris
Production Specialist: Michelle Biedscheid

Printed in the United States of America in North Mankato, Minnesota.
092010

005933CGS11

The Pied Piper of Hamelin

retold by Roberto Piumini

illustrated by Mirella Mariani

Once upon a time, there was a pretty little town named Hamelin. Though Hamelin was charming, it had two faults. Its townspeople were very stingy, and there were too many rats.

There were so many rats, in fact, that even the cats had run away. Rats dwelled in the cellars, the kitchens, the bedrooms, and even the attics.

The people of Hamelin could not live with so many rats. So they went to the mayor and said, "Do something! But do not spend too much money."

The mayor said, "I will, I will! I'll even pay the bill." But he didn't, and the rats remained.

One day a thin stranger in a bright, pointed hat strolled into town. He told the mayor, "If you like, I will get rid of the rats in just a few hours."

"If you do, you will be well rewarded!" promised the mayor.

The stranger pulled a silver musical pipe out of his pocket. As he wandered through the streets, he played a catchy tune.

Out popped rats, rats, and more rats. They came from the houses, gardens, and hen houses. Hundreds, maybe thousands, of rats followed the pied piper.

When all the rats had gathered behind him, the piper set off for the country. As he played, the rats followed behind him in a trance. They swarmed like a trembling black cloud.

Meanwhile, the townsfolk of Hamelin watched as the piper and the rats left the city gates. The people were amazed by the sight of the bewitched animals.

Soon the piper reached a riverbank. Still playing, he entered the water until it reached his waist. The rats dove in after him. Almost instantly, the strong, fast current of the water carried them away.

When the last rat had disappeared, the man climbed out of the river, shook the water off, put his pipe in his pocket, and went back toward the city.

When the citizens saw the piper walk back into town, they disappeared into their homes. Being quite stingy, they did not want to pay the piper for his services.

But the stranger was not discouraged. He went straight to the mayor and said, "I have freed the town from the rats. Give me the reward you offered me."

The mayor smiled. "Here is your payment," he said. Then in a grand voice, he shouted, "In the name of all the citizens of Hamelin, I give you our greatest thanks!"

The piper laughed. "You call this a great reward?" he asked.

"What else do you want?" asked the mayor. "Gratitude has no price!"

"Do all the citizens of Hamelin think this way?" asked the piper.

"Of course! Do you want to hear it with your own ears?" asked the mayor.

"Yes, I do," said the piper.

So the mayor had someone ring the church bell, and all the townsfolk gathered in the square.

"Citizens, this man wants to know if his reward for ridding us of the rats is our gratitude, and our gratitude alone!" the mayor called down from his balcony.

"What else would he want?" the citizens cried.

So, without saying a word, the piper pulled his pipe out of his pocket and started to play. He walked down the building steps.

The mayor's two children set off behind him. The piper kept playing. As he walked through the streets, other children followed. They gathered by the tens and then hundreds. None of them noticed the adults' cries begging them to stop.

By the time the piper reached the edge of town, all the children of Hamelin were marching behind him. Once again, he passed through the city gates. Then he journeyed through the countryside until he reached a mountain, where a crevice opened up. The piper went inside the opening, and of course, all the children followed him.

Perhaps they disappeared. Perhaps they went to live in a new village. But no one ever saw them again.

And so there were no more rats in the city of Hamelin. But there were no more children either. You could no longer hear the noise of little paws scampering through the house. But you could no longer hear the noise of children running, squealing, and playing either.

The townsfolk were sad, but you wouldn't know it. For they were so stingy that they even kept their sadness to themselves.

ꙮ Fairy Tale Follow-Up ꙮ

1. How would it feel to live in Hamelin, where the rats have taken over the town?

2. Think about what attracts rats to an area. Now come up with other ways that the townspeople could have rid Hamelin of their rats.

3. Why do you think the rats followed the pied piper?

4. Do you think that gratitude was a fair payment for the pied piper? Why or why not?

5. Do you think it was fair that the piper took the children away from the town?

6. Do you think the townspeople would pay to get their children back?

❧ Glossary ❧

bewitched (bi-WICHD)—to have been put under a spell

cellars (SEL-urz)—rooms below ground level in a house, often used for storage

crevice (KREV-iss)—a crack or split in something, such as a rock

discouraged (diss-KUR-ijd)—lost enthusiasm or confidence

gratitude (GRAT-uh-tood)—a feeling of being grateful and thankful

stingy (STIN-jee)—not willing to give or spend money; not generous

swarmed (SWORMD)—moved together in a thick mass

trembling (TREM-buhl-ing)—shaking or vibrating

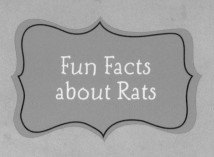

Fun Facts about Rats

Rats nearly drove the people of Hamelin mad, but they make popular pets and subjects in many books and movies. This rodent has a bad rap, but these fun facts show rats are all right!

Even though rats live in dirty places like the sewer, they are very clean animals. Every day, they spend hours grooming.

If a rat in the pack gets sick, the others will care for it until it is well.

Rat teeth are extremely strong. They have been known to nibble through wood, brick, concrete, and metal.

Rats have poor vision, so they often move their heads side to side. This motion helps them see better.

Rats have appeared in more than four-hundred movies and close to one-hundred TV shows. The rat Remy is the star of the Oscar-winning movie, *Ratatouille*.

Space programs in the United States, China, and Russia have sent rats into space.

Rats are talented swimmers. They can swim for up to three days without a break.

The ancient Romans thought that rats were a sign of good luck.

The ancient Egyptians worshipped rats. The Mayans did too.

Twenty-thousand rats live in a temple in India. It was built as a tribute to the goddess of rats, Karni Mata.

About the Author

Roberto Piumini lives and works in his native Italy. He has worked with children as both a teacher and a theater actor/entertainer. He credits these experiences for inspiring the youthful language of his many books. With his crisp and imaginative way of dealing with every kind of subject, Roberto charms his young readers. His award-winning books, for both children and adults, have been translated into many languages.

About the Illustrator

Mirella Mariani was born in 1978 in the city of Giussano in Milan, Italy. She attended art school in Milan and earned a degree in illustration. Her work has been featured in international exhibits. She specializes in children's books, magazines, and comics.